An I Can Read Book™

Adventures of
Arthur

Stories and Pictures
by Lillian Hoban

Including:
Arthur's Honey Bear
Arthur's Loose Tooth
Arthur's Funny Money

BARNES & NOBLE BOOKS

NEW YORK

HarperCollins Publishers® and I Can Read Books® are registered trademarks.

ADVENTURES OF ARTHUR

Arthur's Honey Bear
Copyright © 1974 by Lillian Hoban

Arthur's Loose Tooth
Copyright © 1985 by Lillian Hoban

Arthur's Funny Money
Copyright © 1981 by Lillian Hoban

Barnes and Noble Publishing, Inc.
122 Fifth Avenue
New York, NY 10011

ISBN: 0-7607-7110-3

Manufactured in China

05 06 07 08 09 MCH 10 9 8 7 6 5 4 3 2 1

ARTHUR'S
HONEY BEAR

For Eban and Willa Hagerty

It was spring-cleaning day.

Violet was cleaning out

her toy chest.

She made two piles of toys.

One to keep, and one to put away.

Arthur was sticking stamps

into his stamp album.

"I am going to clean out
my toy chest too,"
said Arthur. "And I am going
to have a Tag Sale."
"What is a Tag Sale?" asked Violet.

"A Tag Sale is when you sell
your old junk," said Arthur.
"I don't have any old junk,"
said Violet. "I want to keep
all of my toys."

"When I was little," said Arthur,

"I wanted to keep

all of my toys too.

But now I want to sell

some of them."

Arthur began to clean out

his toy chest.

10

He took a pile of toys

to the back steps.

Arthur took his Hula-Hoop,

his Yo-Yo,

a pile of finger paintings,

and his china horse.

He took his Noah's Ark,

his baby King Kong,

his sand-box set,

his Old Maid cards,

and his rocks and marbles.

Then he took out his Honey Bear.

"Father gave me Honey Bear

when I had the chicken pox,"

said Arthur. "Honey Bear

always tasted my medicine for me

when I was sick."

Arthur moved Honey Bear

behind baby King Kong.

"Now I will make the price tags,"
said Arthur.

"Let me help," said Violet.

"You can cut the paper
for the tags," said Arthur,

"and I will write the prices."

Arthur made a big sign.

It said:

Then Arthur marked the prices

on the tags.

He put tags

on all the toys

and pictures

and rocks and marbles.

"You didn't put a tag

on Honey Bear," said Violet.

"He is in very good shape,"

said Arthur. "He has only

one eye missing.

Maybe I should sell him

for a lot of money.

"Maybe I should sell him

for thirty-one cents," said Arthur.

"His ear is raggedy," said Violet.

"Well," said Arthur, "I have not
made up my mind yet."
He moved Honey Bear
all the way behind baby King Kong.

"Now," said Arthur,

"we have to make arrows.

Then everyone will know

where the sale is."

Violet cut arrow shapes

out of paper.

Arthur wrote "Tag Sale" on them.

Arthur and Violet

hung the arrows on trees.

"Now we will wait for someone

to come and buy," said Arthur.

22

They waited and waited.

They had some cupcakes and milk.

Violet had a chocolate cupcake

with white frosting,

and Arthur had one

with pink frosting.

Then Norman rode up on his bike.

"How much are the cupcakes?"

he asked. "I have three cents."

24

"The cupcakes are not for sale,"
said Arthur. "But the rocks
are three cents. So are
some of the pictures."

Norman looked at
all of the rocks.
"I don't see any I want," he said.
Then he tried the Yo-Yo.
"It doesn't snap up," he said.
"Who wants to pay eleven cents
for a Yo-Yo that doesn't yo-yo?"
He picked up the Old Maid cards.
"Only babies play Old Maid,"
said Norman.
"I play Old Maid," said Violet,
"and I am not
a baby anymore."

"This is not a good sale,"
said Norman. "My old toys
are better."
He got on his bike and rode away.

"Here comes Wilma," said Violet.

"Maybe she will buy something."

"Tomorrow is my sister's birthday," said Wilma. "Do you have anything good?"

"Well," said Arthur, "here is a very nice Hula-Hoop."

"It's bent," said Wilma.

"And my sister *has* a Hula-Hoop."

"Here is a china horse," said Arthur.

"How much is the bear?" asked Wilma.

"What bear?" asked Arthur.

"The bear behind baby King Kong," said Wilma. "He doesn't have a price tag."

"Oh," said Arthur quickly,
"he costs a lot."
"Well, how much?" asked Wilma.
"Your sister won't like him,"
said Arthur. "She is too old
for stuffed toys."

"No she isn't," said Wilma.

"She takes her stuffed pig

to bed with her."

"Well," said Arthur, "I will

sell him to you for fifty cents."

"All right," said Wilma.

She took fifty cents

out of her pocket.

"Do you gift wrap?" asked Wilma.

"No," said Arthur.

"Well," said Wilma, "I don't
have money for gift-wrap paper.
If I buy a present
at the toy store,
they will gift wrap for nothing."

Wilma put the fifty cents
back in her pocket
and walked away.

Arthur looked at Honey Bear
and hugged him.

He held Honey Bear
and ate the rest of his cupcake.

"I wish someone would buy
something," said Arthur.
Violet said, "I will buy
something, Arthur.
I will buy your Honey Bear."

"You don't have any money,"

said Arthur.

"I have thirty-one cents,"

said Violet.

"I can give you

thirty-one cents

and my brand-new

Color-Me-Nice coloring book.

None of the pictures

are colored in yet."

"Well, maybe," said Arthur.

"But maybe I want to keep

Honey Bear for myself."

"I thought you said

you don't want to keep

your old junk," said Violet.

"Honey Bear is not old junk,"

said Arthur. "He is

my special bear."

"I will give you thirty-one cents,
my Color-Me-Nice coloring book,
and my box of crayons," said Violet.
"Only the purple one is broken."
"Honey Bear has been my bear
for a long time," said Arthur.
"He wants me to take care of him."

"I will give you
thirty-one cents,
my coloring book, my crayons,
and half a box of Cracker Jack
with the prize still in it,"
said Violet.
"Well, all right," said Arthur.
So Violet gave Arthur
thirty-one cents,
her crayons,
her coloring book,
and half a box of Cracker Jack.
Arthur gave Violet his Honey Bear.

Arthur took

all of his sale things

and put them away.

He put the thirty-one cents

in his mail-box bank.

He ate some of the Cracker Jack.

He read the fortune

on the prize wrapper.

The fortune said:

"Someone you love is gone."

A ring was inside.

Arthur put it on.

Then he colored a picture

in his Color-Me-Nice coloring book.

He colored a picture

of a boy holding a teddy bear.

Violet came in

holding Honey Bear.

He was dressed

in a pink tutu.

He was wearing

a necklace and a bonnet.

"Honey Bear is a *boy*!" said Arthur.

"He does not like those clothes."

"Honey Bear is my bear now,"

said Violet. "I will

dress him the way I want."

"You don't know

how to take care of him," said Arthur.

"Well, I am his mother now,"
said Violet, "and I am
taking care of him."

51

"I think Honey Bear misses me,"
said Arthur. "He wishes
he were still *my* bear."
"Well, he's not," said Violet.
She took Honey Bear for a walk.

Arthur sat down

and ate some more Cracker Jack.

He took the ring,

and put it

on a different finger.

He opened the Color-Me-Nice

coloring book again.

Then he whistled a little tune,

and thought for a while.

Violet came back.

She sat down with Honey Bear.

Arthur thought some more.

Then he said to Violet,

"Violet, are you my little sister?"

"Yes," said Violet.

"Well then,

do you know what I am?"

said Arthur.

"You are my big brother,"

said Violet.

"Yes, I am," said Arthur,

"and do you know

what that means?"

"No," said Violet.

"That means I am Honey Bear's
UNCLE!" said Arthur.

Arthur picked up Honey Bear
and hugged him.

"I am your uncle, Honey Bear,"
said Arthur. "I will always be
your uncle."

"And do you know what uncles do?"
said Arthur.

"What do uncles do?" asked Violet.

"Uncles play with their nephews,
and they take them out for treats,"
said Arthur.

"Honey Bear likes treats,"
said Violet. "Can I come too?"
"All right," said Arthur.

61

Arthur took the thirty-one cents

out of his mail-box bank.

Then he and Violet walked Honey Bear

to the candy store.

Arthur and Violet and Honey Bear

had chocolate ice cream cones.

Honey Bear ate his ice cream cone
on his Uncle Arthur's lap.
"Honey Bear, I am glad
I will always be your uncle,"
said Arthur.

Then Violet and Arthur
helped Honey Bear
eat all of his
ice cream.

ARTHUR'S LOOSE TOOTH

ARTHUR'S
LOOSE TOOTH

To Katie Franklin

It was Saturday evening.

Mother and Father were at a party.

The baby-sitter was fixing supper.

Violet was playing

with her doctor kit.

She put a bandage on her doll's head.

"I am going to be a doctor

when I grow up," she said.

"What are you going to be, Arthur?"

"Vroom, vroom!" yelled Arthur.

He held up his arms

and made big muscles.

"I am going to be Captain Fearless,

the bravest chimp in the world.

I have **THE POWER!**" he shouted.

"Stop all that noise,"

said the baby-sitter.

"You are giving me a headache."

"My doll has a headache, too,"
said Violet.
"I think I will put him to bed."
Violet took her doll
and her doctor kit.
She started up the stairs.

Then she came back.

"Arthur," she said,

"will you come with me?

It is dark upstairs,

and I am scared."

"Only babies are scared
of the dark," said Arthur.
"Captain Fearless
isn't scared of anything.
Watch him use THE POWER!"
Arthur went zooming
around the room.

He bumped into tables and chairs.

He knocked over

Mother's sewing basket

and a pile of newspapers.

He knocked over

Father's pipe stand

and a bowl of fruit.

Then he tripped and fell.

"Arthur cut his lip,"

Violet called to the baby-sitter.

"He is bleeding."

Arthur sat up.

He put his finger on his lip.

There was blood

all over his finger.

"I'm dying! I'm dying!"

he cried.

"Quick, get me a Band-Aid!"

"I have a Band-Aid
in my doctor kit," said Violet.
"And here are
some cotton balls, too."

"Hurry, hurry!" yelled Arthur.

"My goodness," said the baby-sitter.

"You should not be scared

of a little blood!"

She wiped Arthur's lip

with a clean towel.

"There," she said.

"The blood is all gone.

It is just a little cut.

You don't even need a Band-Aid."

"I'm not scared of blood,"

said Violet.

"When I am a doctor,

I am going to cut people open

and fix their insides.

There will be lots of blood."

"I was not really scared,"
said Arthur. "I just thought
I had swallowed my loose front tooth.
Captain Fearless
isn't scared of anything.
He has THE POWER!"

"Hmm," said the baby-sitter.
"He should use THE POWER
to clean up the mess he made.
Then we will have supper."

"What is for supper?" asked Violet.

"Soup and sandwiches,"

said the baby-sitter.

"And a special treat for dessert."

"Only babies need special treats,"

said Arthur.

"Well, it is a good thing

you are not a baby,"

said the baby-sitter.

"Because this special treat

is bad for loose front teeth."

"I bet I know what it is,"

said Violet.

"What is it?" asked Arthur.

"You'll see," said the baby-sitter.

"Now clean up this mess."

Arthur started to clean up.

He picked up Father's pipe stand
and the pile of newspapers.

He picked up the bowl and the fruit.

He picked up Mother's sewing basket
and the pins and the needles
and the thread.

"Some of the thread got tangled,"

said Violet.

"Mother's favorite pinky-purple one

is all in knots.

Mother is not going to like that."

Arthur tried to take
the knots out of the thread.
The more he tried,
the more it tangled.
"I can get the knots out,"
said Violet.
"But first you have to come
upstairs with me.
I want to put my doll to bed,
and it is really dark up there now."
"Scaredy-cat!" said Arthur.

"Maybe I am scared of the dark,"
said Violet.

"But I am not scared
of a little blood."

"I am not scared either!"
yelled Arthur.

"Violet," called the baby-sitter,

"come help me make dessert."

"All right," said Violet.

She went into the kitchen.

Arthur pulled

at a knot in the thread.

The thread broke off.

He pulled at another knot.

More thread broke off.

After a while

there was broken thread

all over Arthur.

There was hardly any thread

on the spool.

"Maybe I *should*

let Violet do it," said Arthur.

He took the spool of thread

into the kitchen.

Violet was dipping apples

into a big pot.

"Guess what we are having

for dessert," said Violet.

"It is your favorite treat!

It is taffy apples!"

"Taffy apples!" said Arthur.

"I can't eat taffy apples

with a loose tooth!

It might get stuck in the taffy!"

"Well, if it gets stuck,
you can pull it out,"
said Violet.

"I don't want to pull it out,"
said Arthur.

"What are you looking at, anyway?"

"I am looking at the thread, Arthur,"
said Violet.

"There is hardly any left
on the spool.

Mother is not going to like that

one bit!"

"I know," said Arthur.

"Nothing is any good for me.

I couldn't get the knots out.

I can't eat the taffy apples.

All my luck has gone away."

"If your tooth came out,
you could eat the taffy apples,"
said the baby-sitter.
"Then the tooth fairy
would leave fifty cents
under your pillow.
You could buy some more thread."

Arthur wiggled his tooth.

"It's not ready to come out,"
he said.

"Let me see," said Violet.

Arthur wiggled his tooth some more.

"It looks ready," said Violet.

"It's very loose,"

said the baby-sitter.

"It's just about hanging in there."

103

"But if it comes out, there will be lots of blood," said Arthur.

"I thought you said you were not scared," said Violet.

"I'm not! I'm not!" yelled Arthur.

"I just don't like the way it looks."

"I know," said Violet.

"I don't like the way the dark looks. It looks like creepy crawlies waiting to get me. But if I go into the dark even if it scares me, that means I am really brave."

"Who told you that?" asked Arthur.

"I did," said the baby-sitter.

"Anybody can do things
they are not afraid of.
But only brave people
do things they are scared to do."

"Well," said Arthur,

"I don't believe you.

I think you are mean.

You made taffy apples

and you know I cannot eat them.

It's no fair!"

"She is not mean," said Violet.

"She said if I am very brave,

I can make s'mores for you.

You can eat s'mores

even with a loose front tooth."

"What are s'mores?" asked Arthur.

"You'll see," said Violet.

"But first I have to get some sticks

so I can make them.

I am going out in the dark

all by myself.

I am scared, but I will do it anyway."

Violet put on her coat.

"Watch me be brave," she said.

Then she opened the door

and went out into the dark.

"Arthur," said the baby-sitter,

"you can be brave, too.

You can go upstairs and get washed."

"What!" said Arthur.

"I am not scared

to go upstairs in the dark!"

"I know," said the baby-sitter.

"But sometimes I think

you are scared

of a little soap and water."

Arthur went upstairs.

He put the spool of thread

on the sink.

He turned on the water.

Then he looked in the mirror

and wiggled his tooth.

It was very, very loose.

"I wonder what s'mores are,"
he said.

"I bet they are not as good
as taffy apples."

Arthur washed his face and hands.

Then he sat down on the edge

of the bathtub

and looked at the spool of thread.

"I wish the tooth fairy

would come," he said.

"I sure could use fifty cents."

The kitchen door slammed.

"Arthur," Violet called,

"I have the sticks

to make the s'mores.

Now I am brave.

The creepy crawlies

didn't even try to get me!"

Arthur thought about being brave.

He thought about the tooth fairy

and fifty cents under his pillow.

He wiggled his tooth with his fingers.

He wiggled it with his tongue.

Then he sighed and pulled

a long piece of pinky-purple thread

from the spool.

He wrapped one end

around the doorknob.

He tied the other end

around his loose tooth.

He closed his eyes and waited.

"Arthur," called the baby-sitter,
"come down for supper."
Arthur did not answer.

"Arthur," called the baby-sitter,

"come down right now."

Arthur still did not answer.

The baby-sitter came up the stairs.

She knocked at the bathroom door.

"Arthur, come out of there,"

she said.

Arthur kept his eyes tight shut.

He did not say a word.

"I'm coming in,"
said the baby-sitter.

She turned the knob
on the bathroom door.

The thread around the knob jerked.

It jerked so hard,

it yanked Arthur's tooth

right out of his mouth.

"It's out! It's out!"

shouted Arthur.

He held his tooth in his hand

and put his tongue

in the empty space.

"See?" he said to the baby-sitter.

"I told you I'm not afraid of blood!"

"Well then, Captain Fearless,"

said the baby-sitter,

"you can open your eyes and look

now that you really are brave."

Arthur opened his eyes.

There was a little blood on his hand,

and a little on his tooth.

It did not scare him one bit.

Arthur and the baby-sitter

went downstairs for supper.

"I pulled my tooth out,"

Arthur said to Violet.

"I was very brave."

"Yes, he was," said the baby-sitter.

"Now he can have s'mores

and taffy apples for dessert!"

After supper

the baby-sitter built a fire.

Violet showed Arthur

how to make s'mores.

"First you toast a marshmallow,"

said Violet.

"Next you put some chocolate

on a graham cracker.

Then you put the marshmallow

on the chocolate

and another graham cracker on top.

It tastes so good you want some more!

That's why they are called s'mores!"

So Violet, the baby-sitter,
and Arthur toasted marshmallows
and made s'mores.

Then they all sat around the fire
and ate the taffy apples
and the s'mores.
It was very cozy.

ARTHUR'S
FUNNY MONEY

ARTHUR'S
FUNNY MONEY

To Ann Franklin,
Best of friends

It was Saturday morning.

Violet was counting numbers
on her fingers.

Arthur was counting the money
in his piggy bank.

He counted three dollars
and seventy-eight cents.

"Arthur," said Violet,

"do you know numbers?"

"Yes I do," said Arthur.

"I am working with numbers
right now."

"Well," said Violet,
"if I have five peas
and you take three
and give me back two,
how many peas will I have?"

"All of them," said Arthur.

"I don't like peas,

so I wouldn't take any."

"I know you don't like peas,"
said Violet. "But I am trying
to do a number problem.
Will you help me?"
"I have my own number problem,"
said Arthur.
He turned his piggy bank
upside down and shook it.
But no more money came out.

"I don't have five dollars

to buy a T-shirt

and matching cap," said Arthur.

"Everyone on our Frisbee team

has to buy them.

They have FAR OUT FRISBEES

printed on them in blue,

and they light up in the dark."

"Wilma's big sister

is running errands to make money,"

said Violet.

"She wants to buy

a new catcher's mitt."

"I don't like running errands,"

said Arthur.

"You could wash cars," said Violet.

"The junior high kids

always wash cars to raise money.

That's what they are doing

this afternoon."

"Well, if they are washing cars,
then I can't," said Arthur.
"There would be too many of us
in the car-wash business."

"I know!" said Violet.

"You could wash bikes!

Lots of kids would pay

to have their bikes washed."

"Great!" said Arthur.

"I could get the rust

off the wheels,

and I could shine up the frames.

I could make lots of money."

"That's no fair," said Violet.

"I told you about the bike wash.

But you never told me about the peas."

"I will," said Arthur.

"But first help me set up business."

Violet went into the kitchen.

She got a pail and a brush.

She got a cloth and a sponge.

Then she took them to the back steps.

Arthur was making a sign.

It said:

"There is no soap or Brillo,"
said Violet.

"We have to buy some."
Arthur put his money in a bag
and they went to the store.

Arthur bought a box of soap for 53¢
and a box of Brillo for 27¢.
"I hope lots of kids
want their bikes washed,"
said Violet.

When they got home,

Norman was waiting

with his little brother

and their dog, Bubbles.

"How much is it for a tricycle?"

asked Norman's little brother.

"The same as for a bike," said Arthur.

"But a trike is only
half as big as a bike,"
said Norman.
"You should charge half as much."
"Well," said Arthur,
"it's half as big,
but it has more wheels."

"Tell you what," said Norman.
"I will give you 38¢
for my bike and his trike.
How's that for a deal?"
Arthur thought about it.
He opened the box of soap.

He filled the pail with water.

Then he counted on his fingers

and thought some more.

"Look what Bubbles is doing,"
said Norman's little brother.

Bubbles was eating the soap
out of the box.

And he was drinking water
out of the pail.

"That's why we call him Bubbles,"
said Norman.

"He ate most of my soap,"
yelled Arthur.

"You better pay me back."

"I will give you 42¢

for washing the bike and the trike,"

said Norman quickly.

"You'll be able to buy

lots more soap."

"I don't want to buy more soap,"

said Arthur. "I want to buy

a Frisbee T-shirt and matching cap."

"Bubbles is eating Brillo

for dessert," said Violet.

"Get that dog out of here!"

shouted Arthur.

"He's spoiling my business!"

"You have to advertise

if you want business,"

said Norman.

"Tell you what I'll do for you ...

you wash my bike and put a

sign on it saying:

ARTHUR WASHED ME

I'll ride all over town

and get you lots of business."

"Me too," said Norman's brother.

"It won't cost you anything,"

said Norman,

"and you'll make lots of money."

So Arthur washed

the bike and the trike.

He got the rust off the wheels.

And he shined up the frames.

Then he made two signs,

and put one on each of them.

"Okay," said Norman,

"we're ready to ride."

He gave Arthur 42¢

and he and his little brother

rode off.

Arthur put the 42¢ in the bag

with the rest of his money.

"You hold the money for me,"

he said to Violet, "and write down

every time I get some.

When it gets to $5.25,

I'm quitting."

"What's the extra 25¢ for?"

asked Violet.

"For licorice twists," said Arthur.

"I just love licorice twists."

He gave Violet some paper

and a pencil.

"Now," said Arthur, "write down $3.78.

That's how much I had to start.

Under that write

take away 53¢,

and take away 27¢.

That's for the soap and Brillo."

Violet wrote down all the numbers.

"Now add on 42¢," said Arthur.

"And that's how much I have now."

"How much is that?" asked Violet.

"Let's see," said Arthur,

and he started to count

on his fingers.

"I thought you said

you knew numbers," said Violet.

"I do," said Arthur. "Look!
There's a parade at the corner,
and it's coming this way!"
"That's not a parade," said Violet.
"It's Wilma and her cousin Peter
and his friend John."

Wilma was wheeling a doll buggy

with a rocking horse in it,

and she was pulling a stroller.

Peter was driving a fire engine

and pulling a wagon

with a sled in it.

John was riding a scooter

and carrying a skateboard.

"We saw the sign," said Wilma,

"and we came to get washed."

"Arthur only washes bikes,"

said Violet.

"No I don't," said Arthur quickly,

and he rolled up his sleeves.

He put more water in the pail,

and he put in the rest of the soap.

"Wow!" said Arthur.

"I'm going to clean up!

This will make me lots of money!"

Violet got her pencil and paper ready.

Wilma's cousin Peter

was whispering

something to Wilma.

"Wait a minute," said Wilma.

"We thought you washed for free."

"For free!" yelled Arthur.

"Can't you read that sign?"

Wilma's cousin whispered to her again.

"The sign on Norman's bike

didn't say anything about money,"

said Wilma.

"It's against the law

to tell a lie on a sign."

"I didn't tell a lie on a sign,"
said Arthur.

"This sign right here says
bikes washed 25¢.

And that's what I'm washing.

No scooters or doll buggies

or anything else!"

Arthur pulled his sleeves down.

BIKES WASHED
GOOD AS NEW
25¢

Peter pulled Wilma's sleeve
and whispered some more.
"Okay," said Wilma.
"We'll go get our bikes.
You can wash them for 25¢ apiece
if you do the rest for free."

Arthur thought about it.

He looked at the empty box of soap.

He stirred the water in the pail.

"Tell you what," said Arthur.

"Throw in a little extra

so I can buy more soap,

and I will do it.

How's that for a deal?"

So Wilma and Peter and John

got their bikes.

Arthur scrubbed the wheels

and he shined the frames.

He washed the buggy, the stroller,

and the rocking horse for Wilma.

She gave Arthur 34¢.

He washed the fire engine, the sled,

and the wagon for Peter.

He gave Arthur 36¢.

He washed the scooter and the

skateboard for John.

He gave Arthur 33¢.

Violet put all the money in the bag,

and she wrote down all the numbers.

After Wilma and Peter and John left,

Arthur said,

"Now let's get more soap

so I can make more money."

Arthur and Violet

took the bag of money

and went to the store.

Arthur got a box of soap

and counted out 53¢.

"Sorry, son," said the grocer.

"This soap costs 64¢."

"But it was 53¢ this morning,"
said Arthur.

"That's right," said the grocer,
"but the price went up.
You can't get soap
at this morning's price
this afternoon."

"That's no fair," said Arthur.
"Maybe they still have it
at this morning's price
at some other store,"
said Violet.

Arthur and Violet

went down the street.

They passed the hardware store

and the fruit-and-vegetable store.

Then they came to the general store.

There was a T-shirt and matching cap
in the window.

The T-shirt said

FAR OUT FRISBEES

on it in blue.

A sign said:

"Maybe you don't have to buy
more soap to make more money,"
said Violet.

"Maybe you have enough right now."

179

Arthur and Violet

went into the store.

"How much is the sample

in the window?" asked Arthur.

"$4.25," said the saleslady.

"Do you have enough money?"

"I don't know," said Arthur.

"I have to count it."

He poured his money out of the bag.

"It will take a long time

to count all that," said the lady.

"No it won't," said Violet.

"Arthur knows numbers,

and I have the numbers

written down."

She gave Arthur the paper
with the numbers on it.
"Let's see," said Arthur.
"$3.78, take away 53¢,
take away 27¢,
add 42¢,
add 34¢,
add 36¢,
add 33¢.
Hmmnnnn . . ."

"That's $4.43," said the lady.

"You have enough

for the T-shirt and cap,

and 18¢ left over."

"Wow!" said Arthur.

"I'll take the T-shirt and cap,

and do you have

any licorice twists?"

"Yes," said the lady.

"They are 5¢ apiece

or six for a quarter."

"How many do I get for 18¢?"

asked Arthur.

"You'll see," said the lady.

She winked at Violet.

Violet looked at Arthur.

"Arthur," she said,

"you said you knew numbers."

"Here are five licorice twists,"
said the lady.
"I've given you two extra
for good luck."
"Arthur," said Violet,
"if I have five peas
and you take three
and give me back two ..."
"Wait," said Arthur.
"Change the peas to licorice twists,
and I will help you."

"Okay," said Violet.

"How many licorice twists
will I have?"

"Hold out your hand," said Arthur.

He gave Violet

the five licorice twists.

Then he took away three,

and gave back two.

"You would have
four licorice twists,"
said Arthur.
"But that only leaves me
with ONE!"

"You *do* know numbers, Arthur,"

said Violet,

and she started to eat

her licorice twists.

Arthur looked

at the one he had left.

"I got mixed up," he said.

"You would only have two."

"I know," said Violet.

"Because if you took

three licorice twists,

you wouldn't give back any!

You just love licorice twists!"

So Violet and Arthur
shared the licorice twists,
and they each had
two and a half!